Meet Me When the Road Ends

Meet Me When the Road Ends

A Novella

Dawson Cumberland

First paperback edition June 2023

Book design by Ansley Cumberland

ISBN 979-8-9881419-0-7 (paperback)
ISBN 979-8-9881419-1-4 (ebook)

Published by Dawson Cumberland

*To those who go before; may we dance again
in Forever.*

Swift days bled into longer nights. Sunlight grew shorter and shorter and leaves began to tumble to the ground. Tall treetops grew barer with each passing day, lonesome sentinels amongst leaf-filled ravines. The sun's setting moved quickly behind the snow-glazed horizon miles in the distance. As it set, it took with it the last remnants of red that painted the evening sky before blackness. The moon grew fuller still, illuminating the fresh blanket of snow more brightly with each passing second. All was silent, apart from the few woodland creatures, timid in their exploration of what was. As the doe lifted her ear, giving it a twitch as a cool breeze kissed her short fur, I took my last breath.

Thinking back on it all, I guess I should be grateful. Grateful that I don't quite remember the specifics of what happened. The loss of control, the sound of the tires screeching before a loud crash, then the inevitable silence that follows great tragedy born in solitude. I'm not sure how long I had lain there, not moving or breathing, the tail lights bathing the ground with a red hue. I've come to find memory is a tricky subject on this side of Forever. But what I know now is that pain was simply part of the baggage I was permitted to leave behind for this journey. At least, that's how Gabriel explained it to me. But I'm getting ahead of myself.

As I lay in the scrambled pieces of what was once my car, a hand rested on my shoulder. The touch is what woke me. Electric, as if jump-starting my life again. I rose from the touch, frantically looking around to see two men. One was knelt, hand still outstretched, while the other cleared a path. The men were, for lack of a better word, beautiful. They moved with a grace that commanded awe and respect, which exudes comfort. Once they removed me from the wreckage, they began to lead me somewhere I didn't know. It was during this walk, of which I was silent, that they told me their names: Marcus and Gabriel. Marcus was much warmer than Gabriel, though both were reassuring in their own ways. My mind filled with questions, but my tongue made no words.

Both appeared middle-aged, but too elegant for such an age. This was the first indication that they were not like me. Marcus was similar in height to me, but his posture was very relaxed. He had a full head of dark brown hair that he occasionally ran his hands through, sweeping imaginary flyaways from his face. I found him to be the most relatable, partly because he resembled me more than the well-chiseled Gabriel. Gabriel was the perfect contrast to Marcus in many ways: taller, tightly cut hair, regal posture, and unwavering, stern expressions. I would later find a kind spirit behind that stern exterior.

Marcus and Gabriel led me deeper into the wooded area that surrounded the road I'd been driving. We trekked deeper and deeper until a light shone in the distance. We seemed to be moving directly toward it. Each step took us closer until I could make out what the light was: a small wood cabin whose windows illuminated the night. The cabin was alone, but not lonesome. Smoke puffed from the chimney, suggesting a cozy inside of the small home. A large porch was on full display, illuminated by lanterns on the tables and the railing. Rocking chairs sat with gently worn pillows and a blanket. In the few seconds I noticed these details, my heart could only form one word to describe the cabin: home.

As we ascended the steps, the smell of wood burning in the fireplace filled my nostrils. The slight December chill was no longer a nuisance, but rather a comforting addition to the beauty of this place. My two guardians led me into the cabin, while my mind became keenly aware of the comfort overcoming me;

the comfort of mind, of body, of spirit. The urges of hurry and expectation shrank away, eclipsed by peace.

Marcus offered me a seat on the couch parallel to the burning fire, which I took. Time passes leisurely as I sit there. Both guardians seem keenly aware of the climbing my mind is undergoing to ascend from the fog of its own confusion. They give me food, they give me drink, and they give me time. My mouth tried to form words a few separate times, but none came. Eventually, with my cup almost empty, I decided our first words would start with them. As if they heard that innermost thought, they began to explain everything.

Sadly, it was true. My car slipped the ice on that sharp curve in the woods. But by now you've already found that out. You've been told that the car barreled into a massive treeline and that I was killed on impact. You called our daughter, who slumped into the floor of her living room and was held by our son-in-law for hours, grief clutching them firmly. I've always been thankful for him, but I am especially at this moment that she seems so far from you. You arranged a small service for those close to me and asked some friends to speak. Those who saw you would say your grief was restrained, unobtrusive. That you were being very strong. But they were wrong.

You weren't being strong or restrained but had already resigned to the anger that you'd let consume you once before. Anger that took years to purge and bury. But this time will be different. This time you're bearing this anger on your own. The guardians tell me how deeply it holds you as a victim, how entrapped your soul has become. They have been told the outcome, and it is grim. The anger will consume you forever. That is, it would if I hadn't been given the chance of a lifetime.

Since the dawn of time, communication between this place and your world has been strictly managed and only certain high-ranking beings have been allowed. Certainly not someone in my position. However, times have been changing drastically. The guardians tell me that fewer and fewer people make it to this side of Forever. Few see any paradise. Humans have grown more selfish, more shortsighted, and angrier. These guardians want to do something about it. They chose me, chose us, to try out a tactic never before attempted. I've been chosen to write you this letter, this document to tell you what life is like here.

I was chosen for a few reasons. Firstly, because I was a writer before. They wanted someone who knew the craft. Secondly, they know that I responded differently to that anger you felt many years ago and helped you through it. They know that we journey through our grief and anger best when we have each other. They recognize how much I love you, and how much you still love me. They think that we are the best chance for this to work.

This is going to be an odd experience. They explain they have gone to great lengths to reestablish my understanding of the boundaries of time, space, and matter. Traditionally, those are remixed once people arrive. I have no idea what they mean by this, but judging by their expressions, this is a huge deal. With this time, I will be introduced to Forever in three distinct visits, with the intermittent days being spent here in the cabin. The cabin is in the wood between your life and mine, existing separate but connected to both. The days spent in the cabin will be spent with both of them here, answering questions, and letting me process and write. They mention bluntly that they chose three visits because they fear any more than that would prove too much for me to mentally handle. Apparently visiting, leaving, and returning takes a toll.

The guardians can't tell me what to expect in Forever. They only reassure me that they have faith in this mission and that they are here to help as much as they can. They have a talent for easing me, striking confidence with each sentence. Their words settle deeper and deeper on me with each passing second. Normally, such a momentous task would intimidate me. However, with their assurance, I feel confident and capable. Most of all, I feel chosen. Chosen for something good, something bigger than myself. And I love it.

...

I was surprised when I felt the tears break through the warmth on my cheeks. The sensation caught me off guard. I chuckled to myself, and phrases of "tears being wiped away" came to mind. Yet, the drop rolled down my face. Ironically, as soon as I felt it, it was gone.

How to describe the first moments of Forever. Warmth was the first sensation I could understand. A physical warmth, engrossing every square inch of flesh, swallowing it in protection. The warmth was like climbing out of the water after having a swim. The sun bakes the chilly water right off the surface, leaving it open and relaxed. I have a hunch that, unlike those days, you don't have to fear the sunburn that usually follows.

Soon I realize that I'm not actually alone. I am part of a larger group, filled with all ages. Each bears an expression I imagine to be similar to mine as if we each experienced the same comfort. We were all clad in simple, plain garments that fit us perfectly. It was astounding to see everyone in the same garment, each of which looked beautiful. We were outside a large building that resembled a barn. My eyes scanned the faces around me and recognized some. It was unexplainable because none of the faces I recognized looked like I remembered. Somehow, I still knew it to be them. I saw your cousin Joanna, my uncle Terry, Sharon from church, and even Scott I worked with all those years ago. Once our recognition set in, we began to laugh and hug, thrilled to be together again. Even with Scott, our past grievances made no difference. We were all together and it was beautiful.

All the groups of people reuniting for the first time in ages made a great, joyful noise. It was a loud and grand reunion. That reunion carried into the building we had all been standing before. As we each entered, we found that there were large banquet tables around the interior. Not only that but there was already quite the party underway when we entered. Amazingly, we couldn't hear it from outside; the music blasting and the crowd roaring with laughter. Dishes and glasses were constantly clanking together with the life inside the barn.

Food came in a never-ending flow of courses, and our cups never ran dry. The party went on for hours, eating, drinking, dancing, and laughing. Time passed on and on, dripping into the stream before being rushed along in the current. It was difficult to imagine how long we'd been here. Hours? A day? Impossible, even with the supposed re-established concept of time.

I soon found myself talking to both people I knew and people I didn't. What a funny thing this afterlife is, giving me the comfort and confidence to have a conversation with anyone. You know as well as I how peculiar that is for me. We talked about everything: our lives before, our families, things we find beautiful, and what we think of this place. I began to ask people what kind of party they thought we were at since it felt familiar but not obvious. Everyone had a different answer for how it felt to them: a welcome party, a graduation, a bar mitzvah, a birthday. But my favorite answer came from Scott actually. Scott said it felt like a wedding, which felt very fitting to me.

This celebration was just like a wedding. It was joyous and celebration was in the air. People danced and people cried. I saw family and friends, past coworkers, and acquaintances. Everyone was unified. Everyone exuded love and sacrifice. It felt as if this day represented a death of individuality to bind ourselves together, to grow further. To grow together. It felt as if we had sacrificed a singular self to live as a collective family and to thrive as such. I felt like I had gained new brothers and sisters, each of whom loved one another. I felt a sense of belonging, comforted by not feeling alone.

There came a moment when I broke away from the group I was speaking with to grab another drink at the counter. As it was being poured, a hand gently tapped my shoulder, causing me to turn. I found Marcus and Gabriel flanking each side of me, clothed in the same garb as each of us. Gabriel picked up a drink and began to sip on it, scanning the party and smiling between sips.

"I know it's been fun, but it's time for you to head back," Marcus said with a sympathetic glance.

I considered arguing, considered objecting, considered breaking into a sprint to flee them both. It was easy to agree to this before I was here. I imagine that is why I was asked to agree beforehand. They likely knew I'd never leave if they waited to ask me here. But I swallowed my irritation and nodded to them.

"I always was the first to leave a party."

I think many thoughts, but the loudest among them is a question, asking if it will be this difficult to leave each time, to tear myself away from such grace. Sadly, I doubt it will ever be easy. Maybe they were right. Two more visits could be hard enough. Part of me fears they might take their toll sooner than the guardians think.

...

A scuffed baseball rolled softly across the yard until it was stopped by the large oak tree. The sun hung as it had each day for the last two weeks: high, mighty, and radiating with warmth and rejuvenation. The sky was filled with thin wisps of white that spatially occupied the open blue. The air, however, was dense and thick from the sweltering humidity laced with a unique pollen cocktail that would make even a bee sneeze. But none of that mattered to the boy. This was his favorite time of the year.

The boy had only recently taken an interest in baseball. It was hard to care much about it before since no glove was small enough to fit his little hand. Now that he'd grown big enough, he couldn't put the ball down. At dinner, one hand ate and the other thumbed the red laces, forming different grips with each second. He shoveled food as quickly as his teeth could chew, hoping to squeeze as much daylight out of the evening as he could. He would excuse himself and frantically run to the yard, pretending he was running around the diamond. Sometimes he just imagined all the scenes that he could be a part of: catching a fly ball, stealing a base, sliding home to clinch the game. Even when the sun had set and his mother called him inside, he slept with that little ball of leather.

Daydreams fueled the boy's hunger to play. He had tried to pitch with his mother, but she didn't enjoy the game as much as him. She would tire of it quickly, leaving him back where he started. His little sister wasn't much help either. Maybe when she grows big enough to walk more steadily, he can count on her to play. Even their old yellow lab wasn't much help. He was quite an unreliable little thing. He was slow, with droopy years and an obvious hobble. The boy hoped he was sprier when he reached eleven. But the boy still had hope, because dad was always game. That is, when he was home from work, which was not all day like the boy was in the summer.

…

It's been two days since we came back to the cabin. Two days of silence, save the crackle of burning wood and the occasional clank of a dish being used in the kitchen. I could barely look at the pair that shared this house with me. It was not their fault, nor was I unaware that this feeling would happen. I just didn't expect it to be this strong. I didn't simply miss the other side, I lost myself to it. When I was there, I was more in tune with my own complex of self than ever before; so much so that I had to search for myself again when I arrived back here. I was cracked and disconnected. I'm not sure how to prepare to fight this any more gracefully next time.

Ultimately, I'm grateful for the space the two have given me. I feel no rush or pressure to meet a standard. They simply want me to do this in my own time. After the two days had passed, I could tell the first word would be mine this time. Early on the morning of that third day, my mind began to feel eased once more and my soul was ready to learn answers. I sat on the couch, which had become my favorite seat in the house. Marcus sat on a couch to my right while Gabriel stood somewhat to the side as if giving Marcus space to take the lead on our conversation.

"So it was a wedding feast, right?" I asked, "The music, dancing, and food were like a wedding."

"Blessed are those who are invited to the marriage supper of the Lamb," mumbles Gabriel.

I can't help but stare blankly in confusion. Marcus notices my blank stare and tries a different approach.

"Weddings can be some of the purest celebrations humans experience before this life. They're full of joy and laughter. People eat and drink delicious things that they normally don't get to enjoy. Friends dance together to the music they all love, swelling with happiness. They also represent something we're rather fond of here: individuals giving up themselves to embark on a new adventure, as a new unified one."

"Only, you probably didn't see any brides or grooms at this one," Gabriel adds.

I chew on that idea for a moment. "So we were celebrating being here. What about the unified symbolism you just mentioned? What are we supposed to be unified with now? Each other? You? This place?" I ask swiftly.

Marcus seemed to be enjoying my questions. Not enjoying my confusion, but regarding them with gentleness and patience, knowing the importance of their weight and nature. He answered as if his entire purpose rested on the task. Me reaching a place of understanding seemed to be his only motivation.

"Tell me about what you felt while you were there. What happened?"

I think for a moment. "I felt warmth. Before I saw anyone, I felt warmth. But it wasn't uncomfortable. I wasn't sweltering or trying to shrink from it. I wanted to feel all of it. I wanted it to stretch to my fingertips and toes. I wanted to drink it in and let it warm my insides too. I wanted to exist inside it.

"I looked around and saw the others around me. They looked like they had felt the same about the warmth. It was so comfortable that we probably could've gone on for hours without noticing each other."

"What about the people you saw? Did anything stand out?" asked Gabriel.

"Everyone was happy. But I was surprised that we were all different ages. Some were old and some were mere children." I find myself wondering, selfishly, "Did those children die that age? Is that why they are here?"

As if knowing my deeper question, Marcus answers more gently than before. "Not necessarily. Each person takes an age or iteration that is believed to bring them the most peace. For some, that is the time they consider their prime. They feel comfortable in the power of their exercised selves. Others feel great comfort in their older iteration since the slower movements and deliberation in their actions can prove cathartic. Others, like the children perhaps, find great comfort in innocence and wonder. You probably haven't looked in the mirror lately, have you?"

Without thinking, I move a hand to trace the lines of my face. There are fewer than I remember, but not all are gone. I must have assumed a slightly younger iteration. Embarrassed by my oversight, I quickly continued:

"I saw people I knew. People from my past, but they looked different too."

"Different iterations, I'm sure," said Gabriel.

"We were all so happy to see each other."

"Even Scott?" Marcus asked with a grin.

I smirked, "Even Scott." I reflected for a moment. "It's kind of funny. He made my life at work miserable for years. And you know what? I tried to do the same. I didn't really know much else about him until he passed a few years ago. Massive heart attack.

Doctors said he was probably gone before he even hit the floor. I found out that he lost his dad the same way, only his dad passed when Scott was fifteen."

I chewed my lip for a second, searching for how or why to keep talking about this.

"What else did you learn about Scott, after he passed?"

"He was the oldest of three. His mom took his father's death the hardest, so Scott had to pick up where she started falling short. He got a few jobs while he was in school. Once he graduated, he picked up another. He worked and worked and worked. He provided for that family while his mom grieved her life away. She passed, and he kept working. His siblings moved away, and he kept working. It's like he forgot that living is separate from work.

"He spent so long working and caring for that family that I'm not sure that he ever let someone care for him. He had it harder than anyone should ever have it. I was ashamed of myself for a long time after I found out that I was just making it a little bit harder."

"How did it feel to see him again?"

"I was almost happier to see him here than I was to be here myself. If anyone deserves peace and someone to care about them, it's him. I'm ashamed that he had to die for me to figure that out. But when we found each other there, outside the barn, I could feel his spirit and he could likely feel mine. I'm almost certain that mixed in with all that happiness and celebration, we both held some forgiveness for each other."

Gabriel looked at me, locking eyes before saying, "Thank you for sharing that detail with us. I know it wasn't easy to experience or to try and describe, but I'm grateful you did. And I'm thankful for your vulnerability and trust."

His honesty and candor made me uncomfortable for a moment. But what could I hide any longer? What would be the point?

I continued as I had before. "We all entered the building and there was a party in full swing. We each ate and danced and drank and laughed. We celebrated for… well, I don't actually know how long it was. But for a very long time. We speculated on what kind of party it was. Scott suggested it was a wedding. I liked that one. Eventually, you two took me back here."

Marcus chuckled as if I'd finally said something worth chuckling about. "That's very good. As you already know, a wedding is a perfect way to describe it." He leaned forward in his seat. Almost instantly, his face took on a look of seriousness that found me unprepared, but I faced him without blinking, earnest to hear his words.

"Taylor, what you've experienced is what each and every soul that enters Forever first experiences when they reach the end of their previous road. The people you shared the wedding with were people that had also just passed or people who volunteered to greet those who were arriving. Joanna and Terry volunteered. Sharon asked as well. As did Scott. He's actually volunteered for about twenty-five of these weddings since he got here. What this wedding was was a marriage of your souls to each other, to this place, and to Him."

Gabriel bowed his head at the mention of Him.

Marcus continued, "It is much like I said before. This marriage is about unity. It represents the death of the old self and the beginning of the new. This is a new adventure, one that you will not have to make alone. A new adventure of dwelling in peace and perfection that was not yours, but takes you into its fold. You have broken bread with your new brothers and sisters. You are each a part of one another's community, each a brushstroke on the most glorious work.

"You are welcome, and you are loved."

The words settled in the room, all around us. Nobody spoke, but as I sat I felt something new within me. A subtle, unfamiliar feeling that was growing rapidly and rapidly.

For the first time, I felt whole.

...

A scuffed baseball rolled softly across the yard until it was stopped by the large oak tree. The sun hung as it had each day for the last two weeks: high, mighty, and radiating with warmth and rejuvenation. The sky was filled with thin wisps of white that spatially occupied the open blue. The air, however, was dense and thick from the sweltering humidity laced with a unique pollen cocktail that would make even a bee sneeze. But none of that mattered to the boy. This was his favorite time of the year.

One mid-July day, dad was home from work. The sun was hanging as it had been for days; high and bright, full of radiance and wonder. Father and son seized the chance to play ball together, spending hours outside. Eventually, mom and sister decided to join the pair outside, taking cover under the large tree in the yard. The tree was a large oak, spanning feet higher than the roof of their home. The canopy was vast as if representing the protection and unity that those who found themselves near it felt. Everyone was together, and everyone was happy. Smiles were never far from their lips.

As the hours passed and the sun grew hotter, the boy's aim began to wane. He was never a sure shot, often overthrowing or throwing to the side. But dad could usually snag the throw. The boy's throws were becoming more and more erratic, causing dad to jog after the ball when it passed his reach. Soon, dad's brow began to drip buckets. He began to mop it with his shirt, but soon his sweat proved more plentiful than he could keep up with. Beads rolled down his cheeks and back, coating his body. His eyes stung from the salty drip. With clothes soaked and vision blurred, he decided to go inside to grab a drink. As dad stepped into the house, the screen door snapped shut behind him. He stole a glance over his shoulder to see mom and sister playing under the tree while the son was tossing the ball up in the air and catching it.

…

Days passed with moments, each filling its own space in the banks of my memory before closing and shifting to the next. I would guess it was another three days since the discussion in the living room about the wedding. Marcus and Gabriel weren't the conversationalists that you'd imagine, so the days were mostly quiet. I was getting curious about what my second visit would hold. One morning, after enjoying a simple breakfast by a window tucked in the breakfast nook, Marcus approached and took a seat with me.

"Are you ready to go back?" he asked.

I shook my head, already rising from my seat. My spirit was longing, so the question was an easy one. "What can you tell me about this time?"

"You've met some of your brothers and sisters, the residents of Forever. But there's someone very important that you have yet to meet. But you know him quite well already. That's what got you here." He rose from his seat too, slowly leading me through the living room. "When you are ready, walk out the front door." He made a small gesture towards the door, before stopping at the couch.

I turned immediately, crossing to the door in one swift stride. My hand lingered on the knob for only a moment, turning it as I exhaled. I don't know what came over me. I'd never been so decisive in my life. You know better than any that a hallmark of my personality is how long I could take to decide something. Our three-year engagement was proof of that. I could never pick a day.

The bolt clicked, swinging the door freely on its hinges. To my surprise, I was on the front porch of the house. How odd. I had expected the normal to not remain normal. Of course, I was on the front porch, and I walked out the front door. As I looked around, I noticed the same rocking chairs, the same small tables, and the same worn pillows. There was only one new addition: an older man, rocking in one of the outward-facing rockers, humming a gentle tune.

The man's back faced me, allowing only his white hair and hunched shoulders to be visible. His rock was slow, serene. His hum was not loud or boisterous but fell on the ear as a feather would fall to the earth, tossing against the wind before gently resting on the ground.

"Mind if I join you?" I found myself asking.

The man turned his neck slowly, revealing the kindest smile I'd ever witnessed. "I'd like that very much."

His voice rasped with age but did not betray his instant command of the interaction. It was unexplainable. That passing smile represented more joy than I could have ever known. Never breaking his rhythm, he continued to rock as he patiently waited for me to take a seat in the rocker next to him.

I sat in the brown wood rocker, noticing the scuffs and chips on the corners of the arm rail. I can't help but notice all the imperfections that are present. Chipped paint, faded pillows, squeaking hinges. They are comforting as if perfection in this sense is not the most important thing. Rather, perfection shines through with the used and worn texture of such beloved artifacts.

I stretched out my hand in introduction. "I'm Taylor. It's nice to meet you."

He took my hand in his, calloused and large, giving it two shakes. "Taylor, it sure is nice to meet you. I'm glad you made it. Days this lovey are always better with some company."

He was right. I hadn't noticed the warm breeze that brushed my cheek, or the sun shining over a dancing pond's surface. Framing the scene perfectly were the tall, skinny trees that stood like sentinels. The breeze painted the water with texture again.

"I've spent more days than you'd care to count sitting here, taking this view in. It gets better and better with age. Do you know why? It's never the same twice. Sometimes the sun is covered by clouds. Or there's rain pouring in. Sometimes I come at night when the crickets chirp and the frogs sing. Plus, the way the water moves in the breeze is new with each passing blow."

"Sounds like you've been here a while."

"Quite a while indeed."

"How long?"

"That's a tough question to answer. You know, time ebbs and flows differently for everyone. Especially here. Time is much more…loose here. The rules don't follow as they did before. Days are weeks, which are also seconds." He winks at that last part as if telling a joke.

"That's what I hear. That's a good way to put it, actually." I sat, puzzled for a moment. "I'm sorry, I didn't catch your name."

He shifts in his chair to face me more directly. "Yes, I almost forgot your arrangement. It must be tough, being here, then leaving, then coming back. I hope it's all been good though. Has your time proven useful?"

Useful. What an interesting word to use. So much utility in it. As if accomplishment is the purpose.

"Yes, it's been perfect." I go on, though a bit apprehensively. "You hear so many people paint so many different images of this place, a place none of them have actually experienced. They just think they have, but they haven't. Everything they said fell short, and was wrong in the best possible way." He stared at me, listening intently. Why won't he introduce himself?

"How should they have described it then?"

"That's the problem. They're doing the best they can, but it's impossible to describe. You'd need to create new words to describe the feeling this place gives you. No words that I know convey the supreme goodness and peace I've found here.

"I feel love for others, love for this place. Love for myself. I thought love for my wife brought this project to me. But with how beautiful this place is, I don't want it to only be for her anymore. I want everyone to hear this. I want everyone to have this feeling."

The man crossed his legs and shifted as if easing a small twinge of discomfort. "Time here is special, isn't it? Very interesting too. Though it lasts eternally, each moment has the special ability to feel new. It's hard to get used to something that splendid, let alone tired of it." He paused. "No suffering. No pain. Nothing to blemish a perfect existence. No end to that perfect existence. It's something to be thankful for since someone had to make it this way. It is a shame that so many will miss out on it."

"Do they have to?"

"I'm afraid so. That's just the nature of the arrangement. This place only works if it's filled with those grateful to be here, those who lived a life dedicated to being here. If someone came here that didn't live that way and didn't humbly thank the fact they were here, then soon this place wouldn't remain the way it is. But one can't help but shed a tear nonetheless."

My mind continued to make guesses as to the man's identity. It begins to settle on an answer. I just need confirmation. He can only sidestep my inquiries for so long.

"Why does it have to be this way? Wouldn't those people become grateful once they got here? This place has an effect on a person."

"I'm afraid it's not that simple. When this all began, millennia before you, there was a separation, a schism in the way things would be and the way they ought to be. The only way to reconcile that schism was to make people choose this place, not simply bring them here."

"Why can't you just save them?" There it was. I let slip the first indication I knew who He was. And he noticed.

He looked at me with such pain that I dropped my gaze. He said, "That choice is one of the greatest gifts I gave to humanity. But not all gifts are used wisely."

I was taken aback by the frustration I began to feel, especially since I'd all but confirmed His supreme status. More personally, did He believe that I had gifts used improperly?

"I admire your ambition and heart. It is complementary to the mission you've come here for. Even your spunk will prove helpful," He added with a smirk. Then, His face assumed an expression as if He were asking a very leading question. "So why delay your own reward if it's not guaranteed your letter will work?"

The question hung in the air, laced with a thin layer of my own shock. It's a fact I refused to even consider.

He went on, "Do you think it would have made a difference with you if the roles were reversed?"

"I'm not sure," I manage to say.

"Then why do this?" Though the question sounded coarse and cruel, it was not. His face showed a genuine interest as if He were still finding new moments of humanity that He was proud to see bore His fingerprints.

Looking into His deep blue eyes, I answered, "If there's even a sliver of a chance, I have to try. Isn't that what people beg for every day? Some sort of sign, a voice, a gesture, some assurance. I couldn't stand myself if I didn't try."

He smiled again. His smile somehow put me at ease, despite the tension I felt just seconds before. It would not be proper to say He tested me, but I certainly felt I had passed.

"You're a good man, Taylor. I already knew so. But you should know it too."

Despite the ease I'd been given, I had to push my luck. "See, what does that mean 'you knew'? Why won't you answer when I asked your name?"

He leaned forward, taking my hand in His. I did not move away. "I am me. You know it to be true. And that is enough. When the time comes, you will know my name and speak its power."

I tried to pull my hand away, frightened by the turn His conversation had taken. He held my hand firmly, adding, "I'm very proud of the way you lived. You honored your loved ones, your values, and me. I'm proud of who you lived to be, who you continue to be, and who you have yet to become. You will help bring life to so many, and they will find this place because of you. You are a bridge that I am thankful for.

"I know you want answers, and you will have them in time. But some of them are not as important right now. What's important is you take my words and continue your mission. I have seen the end: it is a mission worthy of finishing." He released my hand. I rose from the chair, taking a few steps back as if fleeing for safety. I looked at Him once more. He didn't follow.

"I know you know my name. Nonetheless, if you find yourself longing to know it, do some searching. Search the trees and the air. Search the howl of wind between the canyons and the animals that roam the land. Once you've searched far and wide, search your heart. You'll find it written clearly there."

Before I could think of a response, the porch door opened with a loud thud. Gabriel stood at the door. "You can come in now."

I turned back to the rocking chair to find it vacant, no sign of Him to be seen. Where could He have gone?

I entered the house, passing Gabriel as he held the door open.

...

"What just happened?" My question comes as soon as I'm on the couch. There's no waiting this time. "Was that Him? Like 'Him' Him?" My hands emphasize the quotation.

"That was part of Him, yes," Marcus answered.

Irritated, I continued, "Was that supposed to be helpful? How was that supposed to help me?"

"Why are you angry? Did He offend you?"

I shook my head. "Not exactly. But He said things that scared me. He knew me deeper than I could have ever known myself."

"And that scared you. Having someone understand you at that level?" Marcus looked at me with some semblance of recognition.

"Yes! Wouldn't it scare you?"

Gabriel flinched at this. "Our circumstances are a bit different than yours, so we couldn't say for certain."

I nod, realizing I had overstepped. "I'm sorry. I was just knocked out of sorts I guess. He obviously knew me like He was in my head." I think for a moment or two. "We talked about my mission here. He seemed to think this was a good idea, and that I would be successful. I have to say, it was nice to be encouraged."

Marcus leaned towards me. "Taylor, everyone here is very hopeful. But He is the most optimistic. I know He told you about how proud He is, which is a very special thing for Him to say. This whole plan comes at great risk. Not only to you and Him but to this whole place. We're at a crucial point. If this method works, it could be a new tool in bridging people here again. Humanity just isn't finding Forever like they used to."

Gabriel coughs, looking intensely at Marcus as if he said something wrong. I notice before he can catch himself.

I look at Marcus, a newfound questioning attitude fueling me. "Can we talk about what He said near the end? Why am I the one to save these people? Why do they have to suffer unless they save themselves?"

Gabriel turns on me, visibly insulted. "You know that's not how it works. Nobody saves themself. They choose to be saved. They suffer because they allow it."

"Gabriel, that's enough!" Marcus booms. "That's an incorrect simplification and you know it. Both of you are just riling the other."

Marcus addresses me again, a newly measured tone creeping into his voice, trying to recover from the first time he has yelled in my company. "Taylor, not everyone can simply be saved. People have to desire it. They have to take a step towards Him because He's already run most of the way to meet them. And your mission is important, yes. But you are not saving these people, nor are we expecting you to. You are giving people an extra nudge to choose their salvation." He then turned to Gabriel. "And you. You know suffering is not a choice. You know that. How dare you say something so cruel. I know better. Taylor knows better if he thinks long enough. But you say something that reckless in front of the wrong person and you doom a life. Do better."

Marcus shocked me with his assertion. By the looks of it, Gabriel was affected the same.

"I'm not sure this conversation needs to continue right now. I think we should break and return to it later if we feel the need."

I rise to go to the kitchen. Anything to step out of this moment.

Before I can completely remove myself from the room, Marcus adds one final thought. "We're trying to save lives here. That's everyone's goal, nothing else. Please, try to remember that next time something gets to you like this. Try to keep your head level."

I nod and turn away. Despite what we said before, we never come back to the topic again.

I go about my days, writing and pondering. Pondering what I had learned, but mainly dwelled on the unanswered frustration that still built inside me. My mind couldn't help but count on the ticking clock: two down, one to go.

…

A scuffed baseball rolled softly across the yard until it was stopped by the large oak tree. The sun hung as it had each day for the last two weeks: high, mighty, and radiating with warmth and rejuvenation. The sky was filled with thin wisps of white that spatially occupied the open blue. The air, however, was dense and thick from the sweltering humidity laced with a unique pollen cocktail that would make even a bee sneeze. But none of that mattered to the boy. This was his favorite time of the year.

Back in the yard, under the tree, the little sister stood and walked a few steps. She had been at this stage for a week or two, standing and taking a few wobbly steps, before falling to the ground. Mom loved to watch closely, seeing if she was slowly adding more steps, which she was. Again, under the oak tree, the sister stood and began to take a few steps. But this time, she kept stepping. Step after wobbly step, she gained momentum and confidence, walking more briskly with each step. Proud of herself, she turned her head back to see mom's face. Surely she would be as excited as she was. Sister was right, mom's eyes lit up when she noticed how far it had been. But this lapse in focus was enough to bring the streak to an end, for sister missed the uneven ground that her foot soon found for her. She fell to the ground, landing hard.

Shock is what came first. Shock to be on the ground once more. The shock passed as soon as it arrived when the young girl saw the scrape on her little knee. Her bones began to ache from the impact, which hurt a great deal. She soon abandoned her cool composure and began to cry loud, uncontained sobs. By the time mom had reached her feet and made it to the girl, a deep cry had already set in. Knowing how this normally progressed, mom knew this was here for the long haul.

Mom scoops up the little girl and rushes towards the house, already forming her action plan in her head. Ice for the pain. Disinfect the scrapes. Bandages. Clean clothes. Damage control. As she leads them inside and into the kitchen, mom hastily moves dad aside as she gets some ice from the fridge. Dad shuffles out of the way, trying his best to discern what happened in his absence.

...

When the time had passed and the tension of the air unclenched itself, Marcus told me it was time for the final visit. He told me that, when I decided I was ready, I simply had to find the door at the end of the hallway, past my room, and step through it. I laughed, knowing that there was no door past my room, but his face made me second-guess my own memory. Had I seriously not noticed a door for these past few weeks?

I rose from the table, where I had eaten about half of my morning breakfast, and timidly looked down the short hall. There was the door, placed at the end of the hall, past my room. In my defense, they had added this by extending the hallway. I had not missed it.

I abandoned breakfast, my appetite vanishing at the prospect of this final visit. Instead, I slipped on my shoes and made my way to the new door at the end of the hall. My apprehension has left by this third visit. I don't even hesitate when I reach the door. Instead, I reach out and turn the knob, opening and stepping through the door without slowing stride. It wasn't until I reached the other side that I noticed the changes.

The aesthetic of the house had shifted. What was once a cozy, wooded cabin had become a lived-in, single-family style home. More specifically, it was identical to the first home you and I shared. The details were eerie: the door that would stick just as you tried to close it, the stains on the carpet from our first dog, and the terrible beige paint that covered our walls. Constantly, my mind asked if this was a replica, or if I was back there again, even after all those years.

Being in that house was disarming. Those walls still carried the same comfort and refuge that lined our early years here while underscoring the pain that came later. Everything came flooding back.

I was thankful for my familiarity with this place because there were few lights on. As best I could tell, the only lights on were glimmering from the living room or kitchen. That is where I decided to go, taking each step cautiously and quietly. I could hear two voices, a male and a female, having a conversation. Slowly creeping into the living room, I saw that they were in the kitchen. This was where the lights were shining from.

I could see neither face nor could I make out their words yet. What I could see was that the woman was obviously older, judging by her long hair that was turning gray and her slower movements. She stood at the sink, vigorously washing a dish as she told the man at the table a story. She was pausing for his laughter, which boomed every ten seconds or so.

The man sat at the end of the table, listening intently. He was likely late 20s, or early 30s judging by his laugh. His body was strong. Even seated, I could see his strength. Soon, the woman's story had finished and he began to tell one. I paused in the living room, for reasons unexplainable to me, to watch them longer. Something about them was peaceful to view. He wasn't animated, but he spoke with emphasizing gestures during the more exciting parts. The woman's shoulders bounced with laughter often. I still had no idea what they were talking about, but it seemed lovely.

I began to take a few steps closer as the man continued to crescendo through his story. I was soon able to hear his gentle, melodic tone that was soothing to the ear. Before long, he made his way to the punchline of this long tale. He paused, anxiously looking at the woman. She was silent for a beat, before laying down the plate she was scrubbing and laughing, louder than I expected. She laughed with the commitment of someone that doesn't care who can hear her. She carried on and on until it hit me that her laugh held something else. She laughed with the voice of someone I knew long ago, with a laugh that was so close to me.

"Mom?"

Her laugh slowed as she turned towards me, a smile still on her lips. When her eyes found mine, I felt a little more whole.

"Hello Taylor, I've missed you."

The tears crept slowly as if they didn't want to take my attention. I barely notice the wetness on my cheeks. It's been years since she could say a word, let alone my name. I stood, frozen in place, even as she crossed the room and embraced me. It wasn't until a few seconds after she began to hold me that I could raise my arms to return the hug. Her embrace was stronger than I remembered. She smelled of lavender and the outdoor breeze. We stood there, holding each other. As I clung to her, I could feel her holding me together.

She pulled back, taking my face in her hand. Her thumb brushed the tears from my cheeks. "We're so happy you're here. We both missed you so much."

"We?" I mutter, forgetting we are not alone. I glanced back to the table as the man who was seated rose from his seat and extended his hand to me. He was slightly taller than I am. He appeared to be in his thirties, built firm. His hair is a light brown which reminds me of yours when we first met. I took his hand to shake it. "I'm Taylor, it's nice to meet you."

The man did not respond initially. Instead, he exchanged a glance with my mother, at which they both let out a laugh. It felt strange, to be left out of a joke that this man shared with her.

"Did I miss something?" I asked lightheartedly.

"Not at all," said the man. "I'm Benjamin, but I guess you can call me Benny."

A smile found Benny's lips as recognition sank deeper and deeper into my expression. Of course, I hadn't recognized him. He was just a boy with a ball and glove the last time I saw him, decades and decades ago. I never saw him become the strong man before me. The man with the truck robbed that from us too.

…

The boy, still in the yard, grows increasingly impatient. Dad was already taking his time, but now he will be even longer because his sister is crying. The boy thinks that he should probably follow the others as well and go inside. But he has to end on a good catch. The only problem is now he has to throw it too. He positions himself in the middle of the yard and rears back, launching the ball straight up. He catches the lob without much fanfare. It wasn't anything extraordinary. Definitely is not a final catch. Again, the boy reared back and threw the ball upward. However, this one was a bit too angled and hit the oak tree on its way up. After bouncing on every branch, the ball finally came to the ground. The boy retrieved the ball and stepped safely away from the tree. He lobbed the ball straight up, instantly knowing this was the one. The ball angled slightly in the ascent, but the boy was ready for that. He shifted underneath, never losing focus of the prize. He followed the ball until it began its descent. He was ready, locked in for the catch.

Dad was trying his best to get out of mom's way, but he kept moving exactly where she was trying to go. Mom had wrapped ice in a cloth and was holding it to the girl's knee. Not knowing how else to help, dad slowly stroked the girl's head, reassuring her that all was going to be ok. Soon the girl's sobs slowed, allowing for a moment to breathe. Mom and dad stole a glance, smiling at each other. Though it was an ordeal, the young girl had taken more steps than ever before. The smiles only lasted a moment.

Interrupting the moment being shared was a sound, a loud screeching from outside. Following the screeching was a dull thud, before another loud screeching. Mom's face contorted into a confused expression. Dad was already out the door, sprinting. He could recognize the sound of screeching tires anywhere. His heart raced faster than his legs could carry him as he ran to confirm if he was correct, that a nightmare had taken place in the day.

A scuffed baseball rolled softly across the yard until it was stopped by the large oak tree. The sun hung as it had each day for the last two weeks: high, mighty, and radiating with warmth and rejuvenation. The sky was filled with thin wisps of white that spatially occupied the open blue. The air, however, was dense and thick from the sweltering humidity laced with a unique pollen cocktail that would make even a bee sneeze. But none of that mattered to the boy. That was his favorite time of the year.

...

Tears flowed freely, as I'm sure you know. I wept, and this time the tears flowed too swiftly to wipe away. They poured down my face, soaking my shirt. This time, I was held tightly, safely in the arms of our son whom we put in the ground. There was a movement in my chest. It wiggled and warmed the parts it could touch, blindly finding every organ and bone in its path. It felt like healing finally reaching my heart.

It took some time before I could gather myself enough to have a conversation, as I'm sure you can imagine. Mom and Benny both waited, not an ounce of hurry in their bodies. We sat down at the kitchen table since they were the closest seats. Mom held my hand in hers, gently rubbing it with the occasional squeeze. The squeeze almost felt like a reminder that all of this was real, happening not in a dream but still dream-like. Benny sat elegantly, watching as I composed myself. His demeanor was confident but also contained a soothing, comforting quality. I was shocked by the foreignness of it all. In shock, I couldn't bring myself to look at him for long. More painfully, I think he noticed.

My mom broke the silence, as she often did. "We have so much to be thankful for. How wonderful that we can be here together."

"I've missed you both. It feels like ages ago since I lost you." Curiosity filled my mind as I spoke those words, leading to my next question. "Do you know how long it's been?" I asked, not in accusation, but with real wonder.

She smirked, expecting the question, amused that I'd finally asked.

"Honestly, no. I haven't the slightest idea how long it's been. You probably have heard, but time works a bit more dynamically here. We don't live bound by it. Our days aren't made to contort to the linear rules we once knew. Instead, we get to live with time. Time is our tool, to use and experience as we choose. It finds you in a sensory way, like warmth from a fire finds your cheek. It bends and washes over you with your will."

My expression must have shown how utterly confused I was by her statement. She must notice, because she laughs, waving her hand to dismiss the thought.

"No, I don't know how long it has been."

I look into her eyes, knowing I have to tell her the honest truth. "It's been almost nine years since we lost you, longer considering how you were in those last years." My voice broke for a second before continuing. "Those last years were so hard, mom. Seeing you suffer like that broke my heart. I felt helpless because we couldn't do anything. You couldn't even talk to us anymore…"

"I know that was tough. I can only imagine the strain it put on you and Carol. Nobody should have to go through what you two had to endure. But despite all that, you and Carol were still so comforting, so gentle. You both remained kind. You let me hold on to my dignity."

I sat silently, remembering the dull aches of grief I remember from long ago. Taking my silence as a response, she continues.

"If it helps, there's many of those parts that I don't really remember. At least, that's not how I have come to remember them."

My mind pauses at this. "What do you mean you don't remember those parts?"

She explains slowly as if trying to show me just how many nuances what she is saying contains. "I was allowed, or am allowed, to make that choice. It's a choice that comes to me almost daily; a choice to forego memories that were filled with pain. These are the memories so full of pain that they flood the senses for months on end if you let them.

"Instead, I can cherish the kindness of a loving son and his wonderful wife, who sacrificed their own desires to show an old woman some care in her final years. I cherish the books you read to me as I drifted in and out of a sleepless haze that my mind had imprisoned me in. I cherish the soft songs Carol would sing to me when she had to clean for me. She was so gentle. For an old woman whose life looked to be nearing the road's end, it was perfect. For me now, it's still perfect. Your love was perfect. I just wish I could have shown you how much I appreciated your perfect love."

Tears well in my eyes, no longer an abnormal occurrence. I break my mother's gaze to look at Benny. "What about you?"

He sits up as he addresses my question. He'd been waiting for his turn, I can tell by his eagerness. "I remember how much fun we used to have together. You, me, mom, and little sis. Even that old dog. Throwing the ball was all I wanted to do for a long time. I'm sure that got pretty old." He pauses to laugh, seeming to remember specific moments. "Mom and sis would cheer us on from under that big oak. Man, I loved that tree. I loved how the yard was filled with daffodils and dead patches of grass, but the oak was always the star.

"I remember that old house with its squeaky floors and doors that would stick. I couldn't sneak out of my room at night because the floors would give me away before I'd made it down the hall. Mom always had some sort of project going on in that house. Sometimes she was painting the walls a new color or shifting the furniture around to see if it looked better with the sofa on a different wall. She made it feel like a new house almost every month. I remember how you and mom knew just about every car that drove by. They would give a honk or a wave, sometimes pulling in and chatting for a while. Guess that's the perk of a small town and living on a main road."

I look at my hands, struggling with the last detail. Though he told no lies, you know as well as I do that the road occupies more painful memories than that. But I let him continue, listening with genuine interest.

"I remember going to school, talking to my friends about my mom and dad, and even my baby sister. I would tell them all about our adventures. I would tell them about the creaky floor and the changing house. I would tell them all about my favorite tree and even about the daffodils. Then sometimes they would tell me about their mom or dad. Sometimes they only had a good one. Or the house they talked about sounded much different from ours. Sometimes they had a sister or even a brother, but they didn't get on well. Sometimes I would hear about how my friends lived when they left school and felt sad. Sad that they didn't have a mom and sister that cheered them on when they had fun. Sad that they didn't have a dad that had fun with them, no matter how busy they were.

"So I guess what I remember is having the best life anyone could ask for. Maybe it was the cozy house or the big yard. But I'd venture to say it was because I had a family I loved more than anything, and they loved me back."

He reaches and takes my hand in his. I don't recognize his strength, his grace. But there is something in it that I do recognize, but I can't put my finger on it. I just know it reminds me of you, and for that I love it.

But I cannot match his grace, because boiling in me is a frustration, one I thought I'd tamed long ago. A frustration born in unfairness, of incorrect justice. I have a wave of growing anger towards Him, who brought me here and permitted me this mission in the first place. But I doubt this was His plan for me, to feel angry instead of grateful. But seeing these two, who suffered so long before, now have no trace of that suffering, makes me question so much. Question why they had to endure it, to begin with.

Why did He let them suffer at all, why did He allow any of us to suffer if those memories wouldn't even stick with us? What's the point, other than to leave the ones we love stuck with the broken pieces, stuck dealing with our baggage. He took my mom's strength, her health, and her mind, and let her suffer with us like that for years. He took my son before either of us got to see this strength and grace that the world desperately needs in it.

I wiped my eyes as I rose from the table. I hugged our son. I kiss my mother's cheek. "I love you both so much. I have to go for a short while, but I can't wait to return to be with you."

"Wait, where are you going?" asks my mom. But I didn't respond, because they could not understand. I suppose you're the only one who could remotely understand. It's the same question you'd been asking for years. I guess I'd just given up finding an answer. Well, I'm getting us an answer, sweetheart.

I make my way to the front door, pausing with a hand on the knob. "I know what comes next, but I don't want it with you Marcus. Or you Gabriel. I'm going to turn this knob, and when I do, I want Him. I want to talk with Him right now." My voice holds raw anger. I turn the knob.

My stride does not slow as I step onto the porch. The sun glares harshly, causing me to squint. The house must have been darker than I thought. As my eyes adjust to the amber hue painting the porch, I catch sight of Him at the far railing. His hand rests causally on the wood, effortlessly supporting as He gazes at the landscape. I begin to walk towards Him, but He doesn't turn to face me despite obviously realizing I'm here.

"I always love a good sunset. That color, washing over everything and everyone, brings me peace like no other. It's like it washes the soils of the day from you before the evening slumber, cleansing you."

"Why did you do it? Why did you let them suffer so much if you were just going to take them away? What was any of it for? They don't even remember it. It left me and my family to pick up the broken pieces. Some were so shattered, we couldn't recover."

He predictably avoids the question. "You know what else I like about a good sunset? It's also a nice reminder that regardless of what came before, goodness can still follow after, and touch everything around it."

"Goodness? Do you really want to talk about goodness right now? Goodness is not letting a mother lose her strength and mind before she loses her body. Goodness is letting a child grow up and grow old, letting them live a full life. Goodness is a mother not burying her firstborn before he turns seven. Goodness is not breaking a heart over and over and…"

He finally turns to me at this moment, His gaze cutting my words off. He does not match my anger, but instead, His eyes show pain, as if a heart had just been shattered. "Taylor, I understand your pain. Believe me, more than you know. But I did not cause those things to happen. But what I have done is try to bring some sort of meaning to their suffering, and reward their faithfulness. Just look at where they are, look at how they affected those around them during their time before this place. I bring rest to their weariness. I breathe power into their good memories and bring them comfort, peace, and sanctuary. More than anything, I tried to give them a place they felt they belonged. But by design, I couldn't intervene."

"Couldn't intervene? You could have stopped it all with one breath. You can move mountains just by speaking. You could have done something! Anything!"

"Taylor, you know it's not that simple. Humanity holds two powers as pillars: knowledge and choice. They have for ages. Because of that, I can only offer my help, but it must be sought after. But it is open for any who seek it."

"That makes no sense. You make no sense. They both trusted you, I trusted you, and where were you? Letting my family wither and die…"

He closes the space between us, raising His right hand. Before I could retreat, His fingertips were on my face, connected by some power. The power felt like the pull you feel as you are placing a magnet on the refrigerator, drawing closer when held only an inch apart.

That's when it happened. That's when He allowed me to feel it.

My eyes rolled back, and my vision pulled back, further from my own thoughts, further from consciousness, further from what felt truly real. I drew further and further, crossing space and void I had no knowledge of existing. In those moments, I lost trust in my own understanding.

Suddenly, I was there. I saw everything as it was beginning in the first days. All creation was infinitely vast and moldable in the grasp of my fingers. Whole stars and galaxies floated around my arms, moving and shaping beneath my touch. Somehow, my fingers knew the moves to make, to form things into being. They knew the right places for the right pieces.

A sudden pull came over me, like the zoom of a lens. The scale was more manageable, familiar compared to that of the entire cosmos. I saw it all at once, from dust to breath. Woman followed soon after. We each walked and talked and shared love. Everything was good. Then man left, our walks were finished, and our communion was broken. He felt the pain and I felt the agony. What did I do wrong? Why did he leave? Why did I let him?

I zoom forward in space again. Millennia passed beside me and still the pain aches. When he hurts, I feel that hurt too. Why do they choose to be in such pain? If they'd just come back, come home, they would hurt no more. I know what would be so much better for them, but the choice must remain. That is a piece of me that I cannot take back, that ability. Choice. Decisiveness. May wisdom not fail now.

I try to send help, try to send signs, anything to extend my hand to them. They must know that my heart still searches for them, that my love still longs for theirs. Sometimes they hear, and sometimes they are deaf to me.

The zoom through space comes again, no less abrupt. This time it feels like a cyclone, whirling me violently. This time, the rushing doesn't stop. As I move through both space and time, I abide by neither. My speed increases as I begin experiencing moments in rapid succession, sometimes too fast to register anything but the emotions they cause within me. Joy. Pain. Laughter. Weeping. Love. Loss. Some were mine, and some were not. Each comes and goes as I continue to move through the abstraction of my own construction. I feel the crisp morning of the first days as I see the fire of the last. Beginning and end are before me at the same time, as if they are circular. I can see both in one glance. It makes me feel isolated, and alone, as I witness both and can not share the experience with any other.

For the first time, I remember myself. Not sentience, but Taylor. That memory shines through like a single sliver of light, slipping through the space between curtains just as the morning rise begins to ascend. The memory grounds me, reminding me that this is not where I'm supposed to stay. I try to cry out. Make it stop. I beg you, make it stop. But I cannot hear the plea in this void, a vacuum for sound. All sound seems lost. No wind rushing, no ambiance of life, no songs to be sung. Even my breathing, which must be labored, is inaudible. Light leaves space as all hopes of sight follow. There I exist, between spaces, in between cracks of reality. A pocket of forgotten items. I can feel no matter, no existence.

I am utterly gone and forgotten. Nothingness swallows my nothingness.

"Taylor, come home."

His voice fills every gap, warms every inch, and soothes every fear. Hope is breathed into my wandering spirit. My eyes open. I didn't know they had been closed. I stood in blackness, but blackness I could see. I could see my hands, my feet firmly on the ground. Off in the distance, I saw the glorious light. It appeared like a small, powerful dot on the blackness of the canvas this space occupied. As I turned my gaze from side to side, all I could see was an infinite distance of unknown in each direction.

"Taylor, come home."

The light, the light is home. Deep in my chest, I know this much. Certainty of any other fact is gone, but I know this is true. Yet, I fear stepping forward. I look to each side again, searching for answers, for anything.

"Home."

My focus is locked. His voice found me and captured my attention. I gaze at the light, not even blinking. I raise my right foot to step forward. Before my soul touches the ground, the light begins expanding, onward and outward. Light fills the area around me. The brightness is overwhelming. My eyes squint until they close, the light enveloping everything.

I hear birds singing.

My eyes, my real eyes, open slowly. It takes my sight several moments to grow accustomed to the world again. I find myself lying on the porch, body mine once more. I never thought I would feel such joy to be back in my body, lying on the ground. That's when I feel my head being held elevated from my body.

I look above me as I stay flat on my back. That's when I see His face, the warm familiar smile. He sits on the ground beside me, His firm and worn old hands are what hold my head. His gentleness somehow surprises me, even after everything I've witnessed. His eyes are misty, and a glaze of tears covers them without falling.

"You came home."

That's when I see Him, all of Him for the first time. Every crease in His hands, each line that draws across His face. I see not only the wear, but also understand how they were put there. I see the palms and fingers that molded with great care. I look into the eyes that have both seen and made all that is good. The eyes that have witnessed that which is evil, trying to destroy the good that was made. I see the way they look at me now, as they have always looked at me.

And I love Him for that look, the way it understands all of me and loves me all the same. And I begin to weep.

"It's ok. I'm glad you came home."

I continued weeping, longer than I expected. He soothed me, rocking with a slow rhythm. He held me, never abandoning me as I lay there, weeping still. No words were spoken except the phrase He kept pouring over me, "I'm glad you came home".

This is when, for the first time in my existence, I began to understand the love, the faithfulness He had kept for me so long. That is also when I understood the answer to my question, the one that had stirred so much confusion and bitterness in me. Why would He let us choose on our own, hopelessly wandering, suffering in the journey, hoping we would wisely choose to come home. Especially when so much was on the line.

He allows us to wander so we would know how it feels to come home.

…

I had understood why we suffered. We suffered because we dwelled imperfectly. In dwelling imperfectly, imperfections have to affect us too. We suffered because we had not reached Forever, where goodness exists purely. Our suffering propelled us further to become someone else, someone new. For better or worse. I understood that fact. Suffering was necessary for life on Earth.

I was angry because I was selfish. I didn't understand why suffering had to happen to mom, to our son, to you, and to me. But selfishness has no place in Forever. Neither does suffering. And for that, I'm grateful.

My mission ended with that final visit. Marcus told me it was time to put the finishing touches on this so they can deliver it. I'm not sure how they plan to get it to you. I just hope it finds you well. I hope you take comfort in it and it does what it needs to do. If you can find it in your heart, don't keep it to yourself. This letter may be for you, my love, but this message is for so many more.

I imagine this might be the last chance I get to talk to you for a little while. Don't mourn this though. I passed quickly and felt no pain. But more importantly, Forever is greater than anything I could describe to you here. I'm in good hands. This afternoon, I plan to drop this letter off with Marcus, then have tea with my mom. Benny said we might go for a walk in the woods as the sun sets. I like the sound of this life.

Being here has made me look at my time on Earth differently. There really isn't a lot that matters like I once thought. Life isn't meaningless, for sure, but it does have fewer significant events than I believed. I'd imagine you'd feel the same way if only you knew.

I'm feeling confident that you've still got a good bit of time left there. Don't waste it. I know that you have so many reasons to become cynical, even bitter. It hasn't been easy. But don't, I beg you. Instead, treat each moment as the gift that it is. Spread love to our daughter and her family. Hug that grandbaby every chance you get. Give her a kiss from her grandpa.

Keep spreading that love, wide and far enough for anybody that comes near. People really are an extraordinary thing. It may not look like it, but they need you and you need them. Hold each other in the struggles, but know it's not meant to last forever.

Have more fun. You and I had so much fun in our years together. You deserve to keep doing fun things. Go on trips, and laugh with friends.

Intentionally seek to live in joy instead of letting other feelings grab hold for too long.

Seek Him. I know you have felt abandoned and lost. You've been hurt and you blame Him. But it's not His fault. The time I've been here convinces me more and more, and I suspect you know this to be true too. He longs to be with you, but you have to reach out. That's what He wants, deeply, for you to want a relationship again.

Your journey isn't over. You still have so much road to traverse before we will meet again, in the glory of Forever. But don't rush to the destination. Enjoy every twist and turn of the path. Soak in the sights, and take fun pit stops. Laugh and make memories along the way. Share what you see and find. And when the time comes and the journey is almost finished, you can meet me when the road ends.

I can't wait to see you again.

Much love, Taylor

Author's Note

There comes a moment when a story is no longer your own, a moment in which it receives its own life. In that moment, it feels like the work stops and the fun begins.

I never intended to write a tale about death, afterlife, and the pain of suffering. I merely sat in a coffee shop one day and noticed a lovely watercolor painting of a deer standing in the forest. That picture now hangs in my office. And on that day, I began to write a few lines. Lines about a deer that twitched her nose as she stood among tall, skinny pine trees. A lake was behind her and the sun had nearly set. The snow on the ground was fresh, having just finished for the day. She was beautiful, engulfed in the serene and quiet picture.

Those pages became the opening paragraph. From there on, I let the story lead, writing about the things we all come to know with age: tragedy can shatter goodness when you least expect it. Pain can cause us to lose ourselves.

Then I wrote about the things I pray we also come to know amidst the hurt: pain only last a few moments, healing comes to those who seek it, and Joy comes in the morning. The weary can have rest and those who are hurt have a Healer.

After I wrote the pages about the deer in her sanctuary, I scribbled the line "…and then I took my last breath". That is when the story was no longer mine, but everyone's.

I hope you find yourself within these pages, whether in Taylor's faith or in his wife's lack of it. If you are Taylor, keep writing letters. The world seems to have less and less of them. Your family needs them. If you are his wife, read the letters. Read this letter. I want to spend Forever with you.

If you or someone you know is actively in the storm of these themes Taylor wrestles with in his tale, reach out to someone. Help is never too far from those who seek it.

About the Author

Dawson Cumberland is a non-profit accountant full-time in Little Rock, Arkansas. He has a passion for reading books much too large and writing stories for much too long. He lives there with his wife. This is his first published work.

Instagram @dawsoncumberland

All general inquiries or inquires about this work may be emailed to dawsonrcumberland@gmail.com